W9-AQM-823

NOODLES THE PUPPY

LEVEL 1

BEGINNING READER · 50-250 WORDS

by Hans Wilhelm

I Won't Share!
and
I Am Brave!

Cartwheel
·B·O·O·K·S·®

SCHOLASTIC INC.

New York   Toronto   London   Auckland   Sydney
Mexico City   New Delhi   Hong Kong   Buenos Aires

I Won't Share! (ISBN: 0-439-77353-9)
Copyright © 2005 by Hans Wilhelm, Inc.

I Am Brave! (ISBN: 0-439-87148-4)
Copyright © 2007 by Hans Wilhelm, Inc.

All rights reserved. Published by Scholastic Inc.
SCHOLASTIC, CARTWHEEL BOOKS, and associated logos
are trademarks and/or registered trademarks of Scholastic Inc.

ISBN-13: 978-0-545-04591-9
ISBN-10: 0-545-04591-6

10 9 8 7 6 5 4 3 2 1   8 9 10 11 12
Printed in the U.S.A.
This collection first printing, May 2008

I WON'T SHARE!

by Hans Wilhelm

I am Noodles.
This is my toy Squeaky.

I love to play with Squeaky.

Let go!
It's *mine!*

Give me back my toy.

Wait!
That is *my* Squeaky.

Good!
He dropped it!

Grrrr . . .
I won't share!
Go away!

This is no fun.

I have an idea!

Hey!
Let's play catch!

Good catch, Buddy!

Get it, Scottie!

Now it's my turn.

I love this game.

Sharing is so much fun!

I AM BRAVE!

by Hans Wilhelm

Look at these clouds!
It's a thunderstorm.

I have to get inside.

Oh, no.
The door is locked.

I am scared.

This is silly.

I know what I'll do!

I'm going to watch
the storm.

Whee!
Here comes the wind.

And now comes
the rain.

That was lightning!

Now count for
the thunder:
One . . . two . . . three . . .
There it is!

That was great!

Oh, the rain stopped.
It's all over.

I am BRAVE, BRAVE, BRAVE!

I'm not afraid of
thunderstorms.